Super Fox and the Rabbit Rescue
is the first in a series of stories
about the adventures of Super Fox

For **Bailey & Baxter**, Love **LB**
For **Noah & Jacob**, Love **CD-J**

Super Fox and the Rabbit Rescue
A BAX&BAY BOOK 978-1-5272-2066-9

BAX & BAY

Published in Scotland by Bax & Bay

This edition published 2018

Copyright Lynsey Burns, 2018
Illustrated by Catherine Deverell-Johnston

Bax & Bay Books are published by
Bax & Bay, Tower House, Fairburn, Muir of Ord IV6 7UT

www.baxandbay.com

SUPER FOX
and the rabbit rescue

Lynsey Burns
Catherine Deverell-Johnston

Super Fox is cunning,
Super Fox is sly,
But Super Fox is of no danger to you or I.

Badger, rabbit, squirrel, hare,
Super Fox is always there.
Helping creatures near and far,
Super Fox is a super star.

So countryside creatures do take heed,
He'll be there in your hour of need.
Whenever anyone needs his help,
All they have to do is yelp.

Self-sufficient thanks to thrown away food,
Super Fox just wants to do good.
Oh, what adventures lie ahead,
Perfect stories to read before bed.

Super Fox and the Rabbit Rescue

Here is a story of a sunny day,
When Super Fox and his brothers went out to play,

In the walled garden, up the lane,
They see some rabbits, the little one in obvious pain,
Super Fox says, "What's happened here?"
The rabbits squeak, "Oh dear, oh dear!"

"Pete the polecat came today,
Into the garden, where we stay,
Pete ran into our burrow,
Down the tunnel, dark and narrow."

"He nipped poor Squeaky on the heel,
Telling us we must no longer steal,
The farmer's beloved carrot crop,
And out of his garden we must hop, hop, hop!"

"You see carrots are our
favourite meal,
They have such great appeal.
They help us see in the dark,
The best time to have a lark."

"But now the farmer's
had enough,
So he sent in Pete,
who's really tough."

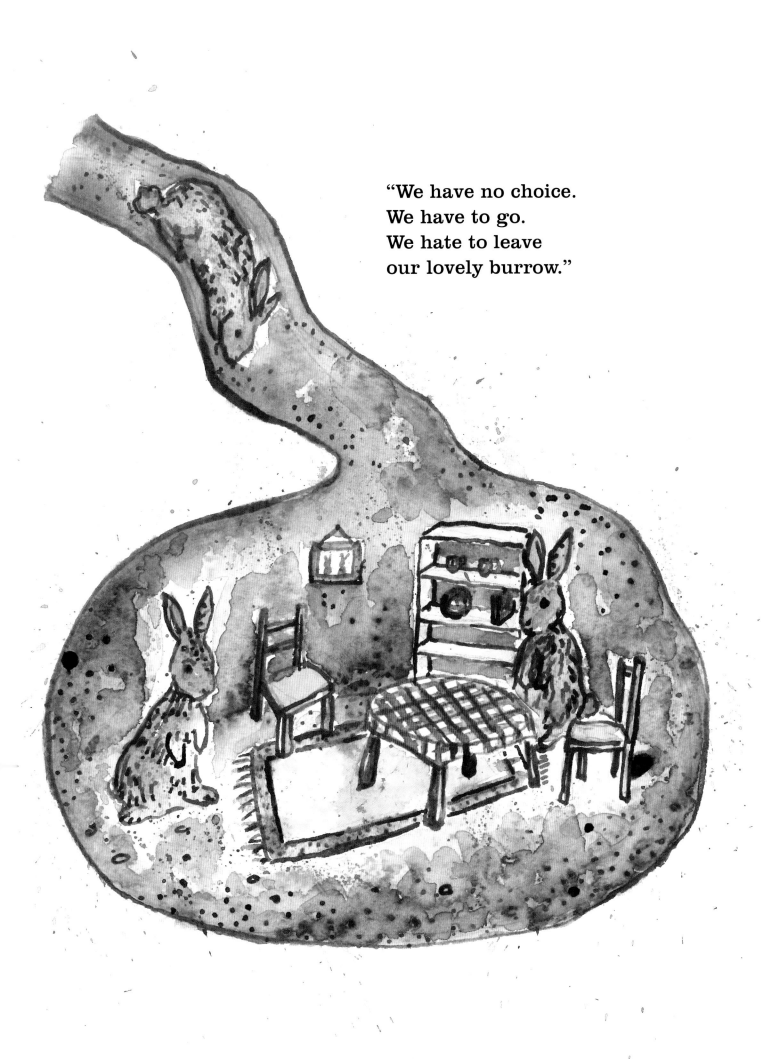

"We have no choice.
We have to go.
We hate to leave
our lovely burrow."

RABBIT STEW

2 little rabbits
2 chopped carrots
1 chopped onion
2 celery sticks
1 ga
2 th
50g s

1 bay leaf
250ml stock
6 rashers bacon
150g peas
½ teaspoon mustard
10 sprigs parsley
12 new potatoes
salt and pepper

Oh what a shame. What will they do?
If they don't hop it, they'll be rabbit STEW!

Little rabbits, never fear,
Super Fox has the most fabulous idea.

To save the rabbits from ill fate,
He leads the bunnies out the gate.

Once in the clear, Super Fox says,
"Look down there, can you see?
Under that huge oak tree."

"The den we foxes have just outgrown.
It used to be our lovely home."

"From here you will have a perfect route,
To help avoid the farmer's boot"

"A lovely tunnel, nice and narrow,"

"Which pops up in the garden,
next to the prize-winning marrow."

"Living outside the garden,
safe and sound,
You'll be eating carrots
by the pound."

"It will give you an easy way,
To get your carrots and
your five-a-day."

The little bunnies squealed with glee,
it was the most beautiful home,
under the old oak tree.

"Oh Super Fox, you are so good,
We're pleased to have you
in our neighbourhood."

"And to know you don't want rabbit for dinner,
Makes this day a total winner!"

The perfect day? I hear you say…

If the idea of a rabbit-friendly fox doesn't seem right,
Imagine if all enemies would just unite!

What a wonderful world this would be,
For rabbits and foxes and you and me.

Just the
beginning...

Hear about new
Super Fox stories
by signing up to our
newsletter at
www.baxandbay.com